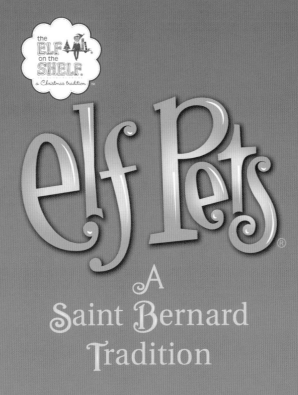

elf Pets®

A Saint Bernard Tradition

Creatively Classic Activities and Books®

For Murry, Taylor and Kendyl

—CAB

CCA & B, LLC.
3350 Riverwood Parkway SE, Suite 300
Atlanta, GA 30339

http://www.elfontheshelf.com

First Edition
10 9 8 7 6 5 4 3 2 1

Library of Congress Cataloging-in-Publication Data

Bell, Chanda A.
   Elf Pets: A Saint Bernard Tradition / written by Chanda A. Bell-- 1st ed.
      p. cm.
Summary: This playful, yet heartfelt story centers around Saint Bernard pups who are sent to families around the world for adoption, with the goal of helping Santa build Christmas magic at the North Pole. Elf Pets: A Saint Bernard Tradition is a heartwarming tale designed to encourage children to engage in acts of kindness in order to increase the holiday cheer Santa needs to complete yuletide missions.
–Provided by Publisher

ISBN-13: 978-0-9970920-2-8

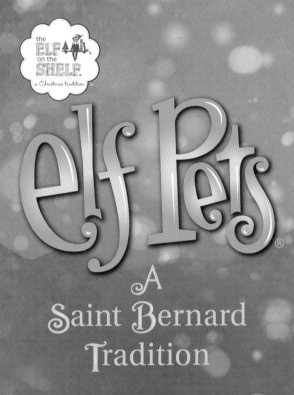

elf Pets

A Saint Bernard Tradition

by

Chanda A. Bell

illions of snowflakes flutter in place,

Each crafted by water and lighter than lace;

They shelter a secret and fill up the sky

As elves swirl and twirl on the air as they fly.

Beyond the grey veil

Of this thick winter's snow

The Christmas Star shines

With a warm gentle glow;

And as is the custom

When clouds finally clear,

Santa's village grows silent

And all gather near.

According to legend, when the star first appears…
The elves stop and measure the world's Christmas cheer!
This Christmas Spirit — of faith, hope and love —
Shines down in bright beams on them all from above.

This moment's importance cannot be denied;
For, without Christmas Spirit, the sleigh doesn't glide,
The scout elves can't fly and the toys don't get made
. . . And the Christmas Eve flight could be delayed.

So every year the North Pole awaits,

The State-of-the-World's-Christmas-Spirit update.

When Santa steps forward, it's time to begin.

The findings are finished, then given to him.

"We've measured and tracked the world's Christmas cheer,
And… truth is, my friends, I've seen better years."
The North Pole was stunned except for a few
Who then tried to guess what Santa might do.

"The spirit of Christmas is deep at the soul
Of what makes us magical at the North Pole.
We have to be certain there's no more concern,
And this star shines brighter each year it returns."

"R-u-f-f!" comes a sound from the edge of the mass.
The crowd slowly parts. A great dog walks past.
Could it be Barry, the old Saint Bernard,
The watchdog of Christmas who serves as its guard?

Everyone whispers and clamors to spy
This great, fabled dog as he walks by.
Some say he's as old as Christmas itself,
A friend of St. Nick and the eldest scout elves.

Their eyes meet. They nod. Then, without a word,
They turn as a thunderous howling is heard.
On the mountain behind them, all the way to the crest,
Stands an army of dogs with strong, puffed-out chests.

"These pups have assembled to rescue the soul
Of the holiday season and save the North Pole,"
Barry barks to assure the jolly old elf,
But Santa reminds, "You can't do this yourself!

The children are needed. They must do their part,
To work alongside you with joy in their heart!
Friends," Santa calls out, "The legend is clear
There's only one way to build extra cheer!"

When the heart of a child where love is most true
Outwardly shines then hope will break through!
"You see," offers Santa, "When children are kind
And choose to do good their inner light shines…

And though they won't see it, each time that they try

To carry out kindness, their light will supply

An invisible trail of holiday cheer —

You'll scoop up and store it whenever it's near.

DONATION CENTER

That light from within is both fragile and dear;

It eliminates sadness and conquers most fear.

So use your brown barrel to lock it up tight.

Keep it safe and secure 'til Christmas Eve night."

The elves celebrate; the reindeer do, too.

Both Barry and Santa have found a way to

Store up the essence, the spirit they'll need,

To ensure Yuletide missions will always succeed!

"Wait!" says an elf, "How does the cheer,
Get back to the star year after year?"
Santa and Barry reach out their arms
Together they offer a tiny heart charm.

With a, "1, 2, 3, UP!" . . . It's tossed in midair
It pops like confetti in cold arctic air.
It breaks into pieces, ringing like chimes
And places a charm on each barrel it finds.

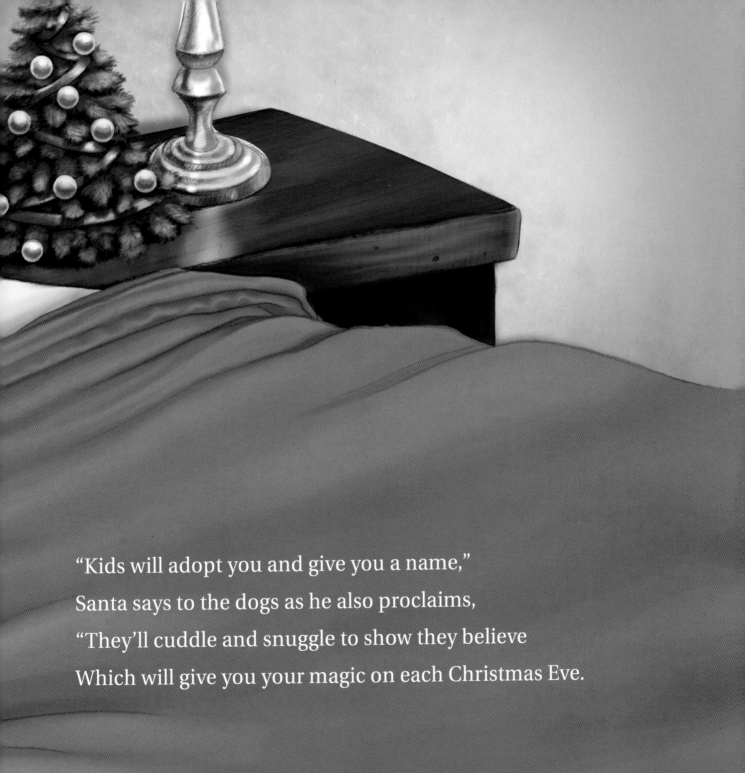

"Kids will adopt you and give you a name,"
Santa says to the dogs as he also proclaims,

"They'll cuddle and snuggle to show they believe
Which will give you your magic on each Christmas Eve.

You'll wait at the window
And patiently find
The star from the east
Watching over mankind.
A beam from the star
Will drift throughout space
Then softly descend
To your golden charm's face.

Your barrel will open.
The treasure inside —
Of faith, hope and love
Will swirl 'round outside.

The heartbeat of Christmas, its spirit and cheer

Will climb to the star so that year after year…

The magic of Christmas will greatly increase,

And with it the chance for goodwill and peace.

Ho! Ho! Ho! I will offer glad tidings and joy,

With a Christmastime blessing for each girl and boy!"

We welcomed our Elf Pets® Saint Bernard on

_____ , 20____.

We chose the name:

_____

We promise to do good
and carry out acts of kindness
to help build Christmas cheer.